nickelodeon

PAW PATROL

HOLIDAY HELPERS!

NO LONGER PROPERTY OF ANYTHINK LIBRARIES/ RANGEVIEW LIBRARY DISTRICT

Adapted from the teleplay "The Pups Save Christmas" by Ursula Ziegler Sullivan

Illustrated by Harry Moore

A Random House PICTUREBACK® Book

Random House 🏠 New York

© 2016 Spin Master PAW Productions Inc. All rights reserved. Published in the United States by Random House Children's Books, a division of Penguin Random House LLC, 1745 Broadway, New York, NY 10019, and in Canada by Penguin Toronto. Originally published by Random House in different form in 2015 as *The Pups Save Christmas!* the Random House colophon are registered trademarks of Penguin Random House LLC. PAW Patrol characters are trademarks of Spin Master, Ltd. Nickelodeon and all related titles and logos are trademarks

randomhousekids.com

ISBN 978-0-399-55874-0

MANUFACTURED IN CHINA

10 9 8 7 6

D0624497

It was the day before Christmas, and the PAW Patrol was busy decorating the giant tree outside the Lookout.

"I love Christmas!" Zuma exclaimed. "I can't wait for Santa to get here."

Skye soared to the top of the tree and placed a shiny star there. "Now we know Santa will find us!" she declared.

But that night, as Santa was making his deliveries, there was a terrible storm. His sleigh was rocked by winds. Bags of gifts fell out, and the Magic Christmas Star that made the sleigh fly was lost!

Santa made an emergency landing in the snow.

Santa called Ryder and told him about the missing gifts and star. "I need you and the PAW Patrol to help me save Christmas!"

"Save Christmas?" Ryder gasped. "Us?"

"I thought there was no job too big and no pup too small," Santa said. Ryder nodded. "You're right, Santa. We'll do everything we can to help!"

Ryder told the pups about Santa's problems. He needed the entire team's help if they were going to save Christmas.

Ryder said they would use Rubble's shovel to dig the sleigh out of the snow, and Rocky would fix any damages.

Skye, Zuma, and Marshall would search for the missing gifts.

"And, Chase," Ryder said, "I need your megaphone and net to help round up Santa's reindeer."
"Chase is on the case!" Chase yipped.

The PAW Patrol
was ready to roll.

Ryder and the pups found Santa's sleigh buried in the snow.

"Stand back!" Rubble said. "I'll dig it out." He extended the shovel from his Pup Pack and went to work.

After the snow had been cleared away, Rocky raised the
sleigh with his truck and Ryder inspected the damage.
The crash had broken one of the sleigh's runners. Luckily,
Rocky had an old ski that could replace it.

Meanwhile, Skye searched for Santa's missing gifts. Her searchlight scanned the dark trees.

"I see a bag," she reported to Chase and Marshall.

Marshall extended the ladder on his truck and climbed up. He reached for the bag—and slipped!

Marshall and the bag tumbled down.
Chase quickly launched a net that caught
the sack. Marshall landed in the soft snow.
"I'm good," he said with a smile.

Once the pups had found all the gifts, it was time to deliver them. Skye swooped through the chilly air and dropped a bag down the chimney of Katie's Pet Parlor.

"Bull's-eye!" she exclaimed.

Meanwhile, Marshall tumbled down Mayor Goodway's chimney.
"Bwok!" said Chickaletta.

"*Shhh.* Don't wake the mayor," Marshall whispered as he slipped
a gift under the tree. He even had a gift-wrapped ear of corn for
Chickaletta.

At the same time, Zuma guided his hovercraft to Cap'n Turbot's Lighthouse. Suddenly, Wally the Walrus popped out of the water and blocked his way.

Zuma had a gift for Wally. "Merry Christmas, dude!" Wally barked his thanks and moved aside.

Over at Farmer Yumi's Farm, Ryder, Rocky, and Rubble were searching for the Magic Christmas Star. They didn't find anything . . . until Ryder pointed into the night sky.

Bettina the cow was flying through the air—with the Christmas star stuck to her side!

Ryder coaxed her down with some hay and got the star back.

Meanwhile, Chase had found Santa's reindeer.

"ATTENTION, ALL REINDEER!" he announced into his megaphone. "PLEASE MOVE FORWARD IN AN ORDERLY FASHION!"

They followed Chase back to Santa's sleigh.

"My sleigh looks perfect!" Santa exclaimed.
"Except for one missing piece," Ryder said,
handing the Magic Christmas Star to Santa.
Santa hung the star on the front of his sleigh.

While the pups loaded the gifts onto Santa's sleigh, Skye took the reins playfully. "I've always wanted to sit here. Now dash away, dash away, dash away, all!"

Suddenly, the reindeer leaped into the air and pulled the sleigh with them. The PAW Patrol zoomed through the starry sky!

When the sleigh landed, it was time for Santa to leave.

"Whenever you're in trouble, just 'ho, ho, ho' for help!" Ryder said as he and the pups waved goodbye to Santa.

The next morning, the pups wanted to open their gifts, but first they gave a present to Ryder. It was a giant . . . bone!

"It smells delicious," Chase said, licking his lips.

"It's perfect!" Ryder exclaimed. "But I'll tell you what, pups—you can have it. Merry Christmas, everyone!"